My First Stories

My Mommy's Hands

Text by François Barcelo

To Brenda, Cheryl, Elisabeth & Sylvie, your hands have cared so much for my grandchildren.

Illustrations by Marc Mongeau

A violin, a bow and the hands of my mother. To Cécile.

alphabet soup™
an imprint of
WINDMILL BOOKS™
New York

Every night, my mommy puts me to bed.
She gives me a hug and says, "Good night."

Tonight, she's late, and I'm worried.
I wonder what happened to her.

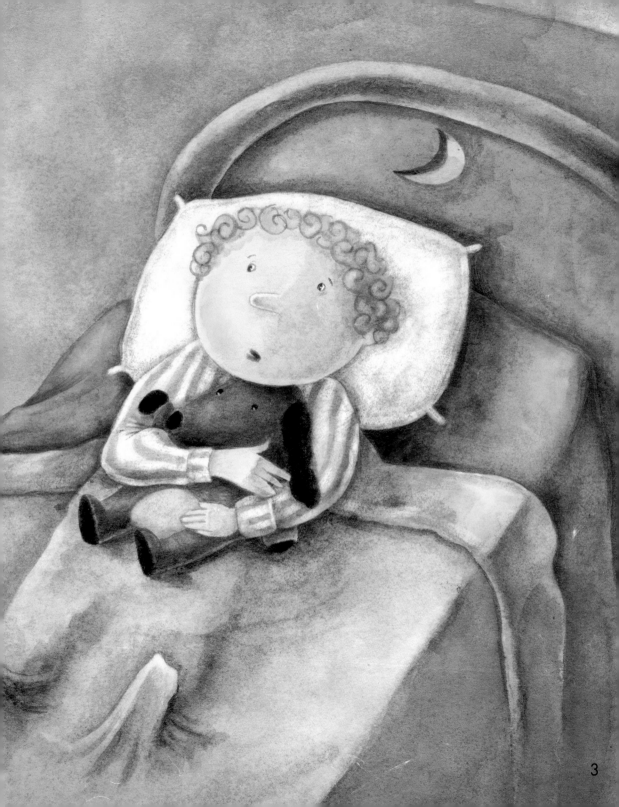

3

Did she lose her bike?
Is she stuck in the bathroom?

Did she go on vacation to a fancy spa?
Is she getting a facial?

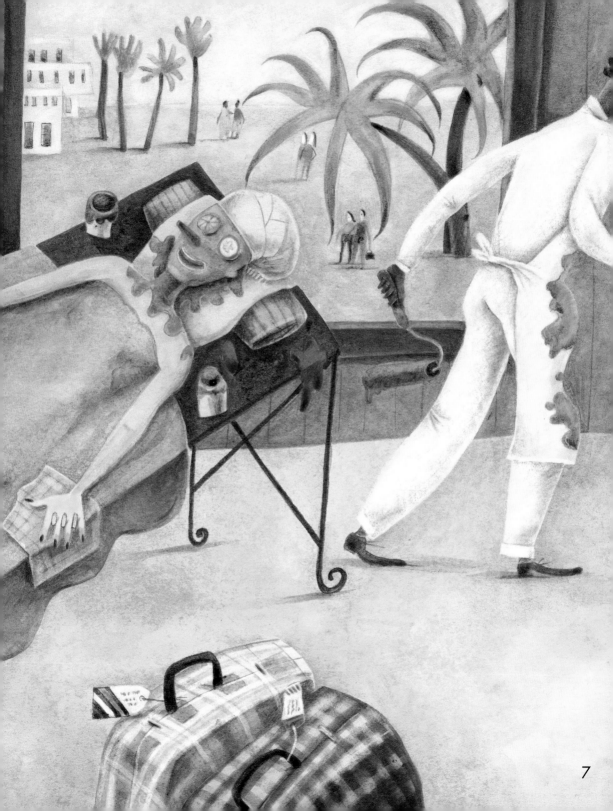

Is she disguised as a witch?
Is she going for a hot-air balloon ride?

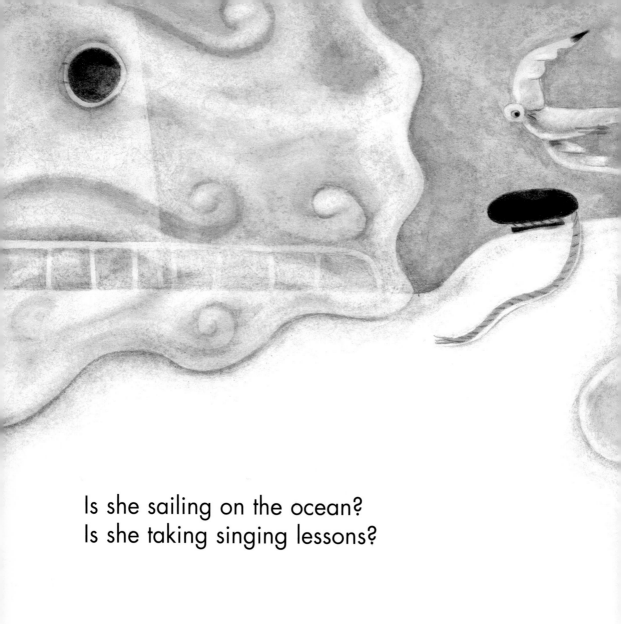

Is she sailing on the ocean?
Is she taking singing lessons?

Did she run off to climb Mount Everest?
Kiss an alien?

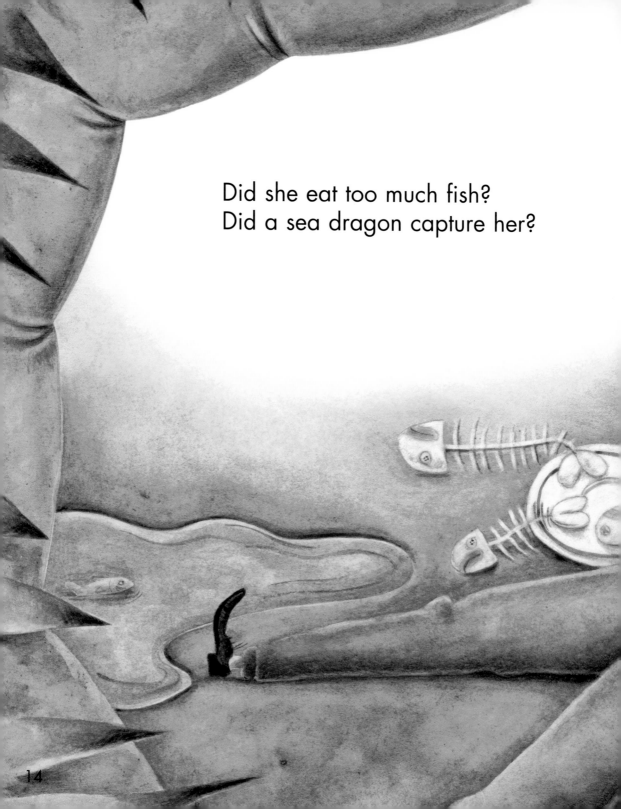

Did she eat too much fish?
Did a sea dragon capture her?

Did she travel back in time to the Middle Ages?
Is she seeing mirages in a desert?

Has she become an artist?
Did she forget . . . that I exist?

Oh! I hear the doorknob turning.
Who could it be? I think I know . . .

21

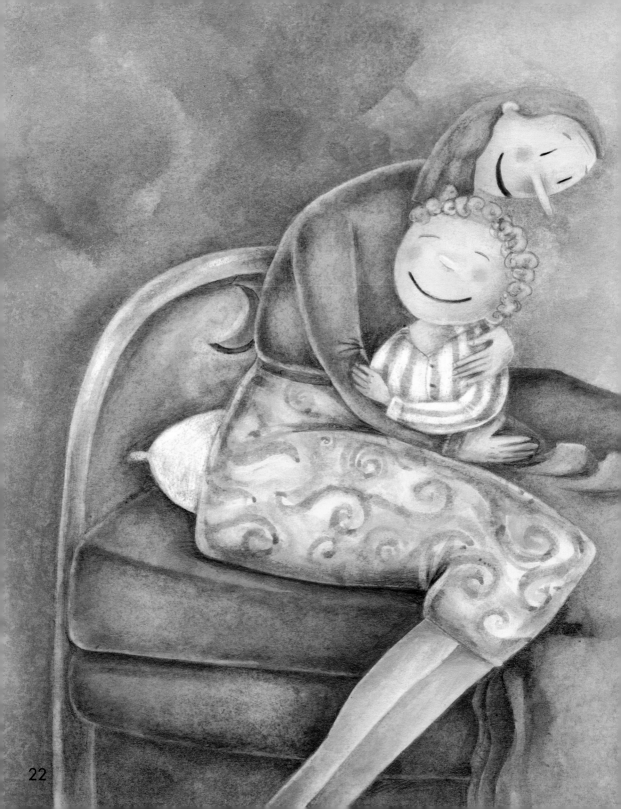

Those hands that hug me tight,
are the hands . . . of my mommy!

Published in 2010 by Windmill Books, LLC
303 Park Avenue South, Suite # 1280, New York, NY 10010-3657

Adaptations to North American Edition © 2010 Windmill Books

Original title: Les mains de ma maman
Original Publisher: Les éditions Imagine inc

Publisher Cataloging in Publication

Barcelo, François, 1941-
        My mommy's hands. – North American ed. / text by François Barcelo ; illustrations by Marc
Mongeau.
p. cm. – (My first stories)
Summary: A little boy imagines all the things that might keep his mommy from tucking him in at
bedtime.
ISBN 978-1-60754-362-6 (lib.) – ISBN 978-1-60754-365-7 (pbk.)
ISBN 978-1-60754-366-4 (6-pack)
        1. Bedtime—Juvenile fiction   2. Mother and child—Juvenile fiction
3. Imagination—Juvenile fiction   [1. Bedtime—Fiction   2. Mother and child—Fiction   3. Imagination—Fiction   4. Worry—Fiction]   I. Mongeau, Marc   II. Title   III. Series
        [E]—dc22

Printed in the United States of America